Hex the Halls

MADELEINE ELIOT

To my alpha team, for a year of incredible support, assistance, patience, and praise:

You are all good girls.

Contents

Chapter 1

THREE DAYS UNTIL CHRISTMAS

ALEC ASHCROFT WAS NOT only going to be the death of my career—he was going to be the reason I would be convicted of murder and never see my family again.

Or my cat.

Not only was he completely derailing my research on ancient methods of portomancy by punching holes in all of my translations, but he was actively undermining my work to my doctoral advisor, and I had had enough.

I was going to turn him into a toad. Or maybe hex him so the ridiculous flannel shirts he wore beneath his robes strangled him. Or maybe I'd push him into one of his beloved portals and hope he ended up somewhere without oxygen.

Space would do. Maybe Mars.

Visions of murdering my arch-rival aside, I had no complaints about my studies at the Academy. Known only by its somewhat non-descriptive name, it was the premier institute for magical research in the country. I only had one semester left of the PhD program. If I could just graduate without earning a life sentence in a magical prison for murdering a colleague, I'd never have to see Alec's stupid, annoyingly handsome face again.

I sighed, sipping my hazelnut latte as Binx meowed grumpily from inside the tote bag I'd slung over my shoulder. I looked down, frowning at my black feline familiar. He was named after the cat in my favorite Halloween movie and had a habit of making his opinions known despite being unable to speak.

Right now, he was complaining about the indignity of being carried in a tote bag.

"If you want to freeze your paws off, I'll happily put you down," I told him, giving him an arch look. "You're heavy, and I'll gladly let you walk."

Binx meowed again, settling down in the bag and accepting his fate.

"That's what I thought," I said, sipping the toasty warm beverage again, which melted some of the frost that seemed to be creeping into my bones from the chilly December air.

I'd chosen my outfit that day carefully, picking my most subdued sweater and slacks and brushing my caramel hair into a high ponytail that I hoped came across as professional. Christmas was in three days, and I just had to submit the sources from my paper to my advisor as proof that Alec was wrong about my translation of the Celtic portomancy texts. Then I could enjoy two glorious weeks of freedom from academia.

Mom and Dad were expecting me, and my bags were all packed and waiting in my tiny, freezing apartment. After I cleared up this nonsense, I would summon a portal to take me home.

I would not be sad to trade the cold isolation of academic life for the cozy sounds and smells of home and family. Mom always put extra cinnamon in the cauldron brew this time of year, and Dad insisted on burning a Yule log in honor of the Old Gods, despite the fact that none of us did much in the way of pagan worship the rest of the year.

My sisters and I would spend Christmas Eve surreptitiously filling each other's stockings with the most ridiculous charms and amulets we could find, and Binx would get to play with their familiars, a rather irritable older cat and a large, slimy toad that my younger sister insisted was, "adorbs."

But before that magic could begin, I had to face Alec one last time. He always stayed at the Academy over holidays, claiming his work was too important to leave for frivolous vacations. The man was a grinch if I ever saw one, and I was more than a little surprised he didn't insist on keeping all the doctoral candidates there with him to partake in his misery.

At least Casimir had my back. He was the other postdoc in our department and the polar opposite of Alec. Where Alec was cold and terse, Cas was friendly and talkative. Perhaps a bit *too* friendly, but still better than the alternative. He had verified my translations himself, and I knew he would vouch for me, even though Alec seemed determined to ruin me.

The campus was empty this close to Christmas. All of the undergrads and other grad students had left at the end of finals, and only a few professors and postdocs were still around to keep the Academy running while everyone else celebrated.

The building was old and imbued with so much magic that the very stones sometimes got their own ideas about what it meant to be a wall or a floor. A constant magical presence was required to stop the whole building from mutiny, and postdocs usually drew straws to decide who was stuck babysitting the building and keeping the walls in check.

Alec always volunteered to watch over our department, and I felt a little sad for him in spite of myself, alone with his stupid ferret as his only companion. Even Dr. Dvaran, my eccentric doctoral advisor and head of the portomancy department, went home to India for the holidays.

I could do this. I could be kind. It was Christmas, and even my arch-nemesis deserved kindness around the holidays.

I steeled myself, pushing open the big wooden doors and marching up the stairs to the laboratory. I would be civil and polite. I would simply leave my references for Dr. Dvaran and say goodbye to Alec on my way out; no murder, no jail time, home in less than an hour for Christmas.

What could possibly go wrong?

Alec was, as expected, in the lab when Binx and I made it up the stone staircase. His familiar, a scraggly white ferret named Max, was curled around his neck as he poured over some document with his back turned toward the door. An open portal was swirling next to him, vibrant colors flickering at the edges of a deep blue swirl as he mumbled ancient words over it.

I pursed my lips, trying to ignore his muscular shoulders. Usually, our required robes hid his frame, but dispensing with them must be his only concession to the holiday. His boring flannel shirt made his breadth obvious, and my stomach swooped involuntarily. How in the hells did a postdoc get so built when he spent all of his free time working?

Dr. Dvaran wasn't with him, and I wondered if I could sneak past Alec without him noticing me to get to his office on the other side of the room.

"Morning, Sage," Alec said without turning, his voice distant as he focused on his work. I wasn't sure how he always seemed to know when I was around, like some weird Sage-detector, but he did. "Dr. D is already gone."

"What?" I gasped, almost dropping the bag with Binx in it. He meowed angrily, and I put the bag down gently. "What do you mean he's gone?"

"He left for India three hours ago," Alec said, finally turning and scrubbing a hand through his hair.

Gods, something about men with messy hair did things to me, and I squelched down the feeling. This was Alec. Dr. Ashcroft. I didn't like him or his stupid amazing shoulders.

"But he agreed to meet me," I argued, shifting the file with my sources to my other hand in agitation.

Alec shrugged as if he couldn't be bothered with my problems, turning back around to his work.

Anger pulsed through me at his cavalier attitude, and I stomped over to physically spin him to face me. He looked down at me, a brow raised as if I were a mildly annoying insect he was being forced to study.

"With respect, Dr. Ashcroft, this is *your* fault," I accused, smacking the file against his chest in a way that was totally *not* respectful. "You undermined me and made him question my translations."

Alec furrowed his brows and narrowed his eyes as he grabbed the file, holding it out of reach so I couldn't hit him with it again. "Sage, I truly have no idea what you are talking about," he drawled. "I have not spoken to Dr. D about your recent work."

"That's a bald-faced lie," I accused, stepping back and throwing up my hands. "Casimir told me it was you who disagreed with my translation."

"*Casimir*?" he asked, eyes narrowing even more with suspicion. "How—"

It was at this moment that Binx, who had been prowling silently toward us with his eyes on the ferret, decided to pounce. He leapt onto Alec's back, making Max screech loudly and scurry down his master's body.

Alec yelled and staggered, pushing Binx off him, which made me cry out in turn as the ferret and the cat both leapt onto me.

I fell backward, the world seeming to stretch and spin in slow motion as Alec, one hand still grasping my files, reached out his other to catch me. The ferret, the cat, Alec, and I all fell through the portal, its borders flashing red as a destination was chosen.

Portal magic was finicky. Without a clear destination in mind, a traveler could become stuck between the fabrics of the universe.

Clearly, one of us had pulled a location out of our heads in time to direct the portal, and while I was grateful not to be trapped in nothingness, it became clear very quickly that it had been Alec's mind that had determined the location rather than mine.

We landed with a thump, the cat howling and the ferret screeching as it scurried away, and Alec's hard body sprawled atop mine on a cold, stone floor.

The portal closed with a snap, and Alec cursed loudly, scrambling off me.

I groaned, looking up to see darkened walls of a wood cabin, the gray stone floor beneath me part of some kitchen. Snow was outside the windows, but not the gentle swirling of a Christmas card. This was the howling torrent of a full-on winter storm, and I could see snow piled up what must be several feet outside the cabin.

"Where are we?" I groaned, pushing up from the floor and feeling my ankle crumple beneath me. I cried out in agony, and Alec caught me before I fell, swearing again.

"Fucking screwed," he replied.

Chapter 2

THREE DAYS UNTIL CHRISTMAS

"No service," Alec growled, dropping the old-fashioned handset phone back on the receiver. "And my cell is in the lab."

He plopped down on the red plaid sofa next to me, dropping his head in his hands. I winced as he jostled my ankle, which I hoped was sprained rather than broken.

"I have no cell service," I replied, frowning down at my phone, which was basically a high-tech brick without data or internet. With all the magic available to the witches and wizards of the world, you would think we might have come up with a way to bypass batteries or cell towers. "Can you reverse the portal?"

"No," he snapped, looking up at me and scowling like it was somehow my fault we ended up in this ridiculous situation. "There's only a single damn leyline here. The nearest convergence is at least five miles away."

"Shit," I said, wincing at the bleak reality of our situation.

Leylines were conduits of all magical energy. They criss-crossed the world, carrying and conducting magic from one convergence to the next, and any witch or wizard could harness them for any kind of magic.

I was studying the use of portal magic—or portomancy—throughout history, specifically in the early Middle Ages. There were thousands of leylines at the Academy to study and draw from, making it one of the best institutions in the world for portomancy research.

Portals required a convergence of lines, but only one line was required to travel *between* destinations. The trick was knowing where lines converged so that one could return to one's place of origin. If the closest convergence was five miles away, we were indeed fucking screwed.

"Well, you got us into this!" I snapped, poking my finger into his flannel-clad chest. It was very solid, and I was a bit taken aback.

Focus, Sage. Don't get distracted by perfect pecs.

"So you'd better find a way to get us out," I finished, crossing my arms and leaning back against the sofa.

"I had nothing to do with getting us into this," Alec replied, his tone steely. "It was you who pulled me into an unstable portal."

"I fell," I corrected, indignation rising, "because I tripped over your stupid, fat rat into *your* portal."

"He's a ferret," Alec corrected, sounding furious as the unfeeling mask of Dr. Ashcroft slipped under stress. "And he was in the way because *your* menace of a cat was chasing him," he added, anger tinging his tan cheeks pink. "I was trying to catch you."

"So this is *my* fault?" I scoffed, trying to give him my most scathing look. "You think I *wanted* to get trapped with you in an isolated cabin in the middle of a snowstorm in who-knows-where with no chance of magicking ourselves back?"

"Believe me," he said, his voice cold as he looked down at me, "this was not how I wanted to spend *my* Christmas either."

"You cannot be telling me we are trapped here until Christmas," I replied, blood draining from my face in horror. "I have to get home. My family is expecting me."

"Lucky you," he drawled, tilting his head back to rest on the sofa so he was staring up at the wood beams of the ceiling. "But unless you can think of a way to travel five miles in ten feet of snow and a howling blizzard," he added, gesturing to the storm outside, "we're stuck here."

"And where exactly *is* here?" I asked, looking around the dark cabin. It was freezing, and I shivered. The winter coat I wore at the Academy was perfect for light frost and temperate winters, but not nearly enough for snow.

Alec threw a wool blanket at me, and I raised a brow in surprise. "It's my family's cabin," he replied dryly, frowning as I pulled the blanket around my shoulders. "It was the first place that popped into my mind when we fell. I figured it beat being trapped between universes."

"At least there are leylines between universes," I grumbled, lamenting the lack of magical pathways intersecting the cabin. "Why would your family build a cabin so far from a convergence?"

I looked around, not made any more confident by what I saw. There was dust over everything, and the cabin had clearly not been visited for years. If we didn't kill each other while trapped here, we would definitely starve instead.

"Because my parents didn't want to be bothered by unwelcome guests," Alec replied, rising from the couch. "We have firewood so we won't freeze. Let me check if the fridge still works."

"This place looks abandoned," I pointed out, twisting to watch him as he placed logs in the empty hearth and channeled a fire to catch. Simple elemental magic only required one leyline, but it would become easily exhausted. We'd have to use our magic carefully. "There's no way there's any food that's edible."

"The fridge, freezer, and pantry are enchanted," he replied, crossing to the kitchen to open the stainless steel door. A warm yellow glow lit his face, which looked vaguely panicked. He held up a Tupperware container, eyeing the contents warily. "Food can't go bad. Doesn't mean there's anything worth eating, though."

Alec opened the freezer next, rummaging around until he found whatever he was looking for, grunting in triumph as he produced an ice pack. "Put that on your ankle," he said, tossing me the ice. "I want to take inventory before using up the leyline on healing it. And I have to find your blasted cat and my ferret. If Max has been eaten, I'm going to be very annoyed."

"Binx has better taste than to stoop so low as to eat your rat," I said haughtily, settling the ice pack on my ankle. I sighed as it relieved the throbbing pain.

Alec rolled his eyes as he started shouting for the animals.

Secretly, I hoped Binx hadn't really eaten the ferret. Familiars could be replaced, but it didn't happen often. While not inherently magical, animals were good at sniffing out leylines, and familiars made a witch or wizard's job significantly easier. Their lives became tied to the witch or wizard who bonded to them, and it destroyed a part of you if you lost your familiar.

A yowl told me that Binx had been discovered, and within seconds, he shot up onto the couch to snuggle beneath my blanket with me. I stroked his head.

"Did that horrible rat scare you, my sweet?" I cooed, stroking his head soothingly.

A grumbling told me Alec was returning, and I turned to see the little white monster curled around his neck.

"Served him right if he did," Alec said, scratching the ferret, who snuggled closer. It would have been adorable had it been any other man, but I reminded myself again that Alec was actively trying to destroy my career.

"So what's the plan?" I asked, trying to keep my tone civil and professional despite my frustration. Under different circumstances, this cabin would be lovely. Romantic, even, with the blazing fire and cozy furniture. With Alec, it was destined to be a nightmare. "Do we hike? Is there a car we can take?"

"We're not going anywhere, Sage," Alec replied, pinning me with an incredulous stare. "You're in no shape to hike five miles in *good* weather, let alone in ten feet of snow, and the Jeep won't be able to drive in these conditions. There's not enough ley magic around to melt a path quickly, and trying it would drain us and the leyline."

"So what?" I started to panic as I thought of my parents and sisters at home, worrying when I didn't show up. "We're just stuck here?"

"Yup," he replied, still looking at me seriously. "Unless you can think of a way to magic us out of this."

"I need to send a message to my family," I said, dropping my foot to the floor and wincing as I tried to stand. "I need paper and a pen."

Alec lifted my leg back on the table. "Gods above, you are single-minded," he relented, standing and moving toward a desk in the far corner of the cabin. He rummaged through the drawers, producing a piece of paper and pen. "Here," he said, handing them to me. "Although I don't know how you think you're going to get it to them with only a single leyline at your disposal."

"I'll use wind," I said confidently, taking the pen and paper without thanks. "Won't you have people worrying about you when you don't show up on Christmas?"

"No," he replied. His expression was unreadable, and I waited for further explanation.

When none came, I sighed and scribbled a hurried note on the paper. "Do you have a leyline map here?" I asked, checking my phone to see if I could access Leyze. The leyline map app showed every available leyline in a GPS network covering the earth, and it was ten times easier than trying to feel out the lines using magic or a traditional map.

The app wouldn't even load.

"Somewhere around here," Alec replied, groaning as he stood again. Binx hissed at the ferret, who seemed to have recovered from their scuffle and practically preened from the safety of his perch on his master's shoulders. "Keep that beast away from Max."

"Gladly," I replied, holding fast to Binx to prevent him from pouncing again. I folded the note into an inelegant paper plane, hoping there would be a simple route to my parents' house. I had no idea where we were, but there were three lines that ran beneath their home, so I knew I could find a path if I planned carefully.

Witches and wizards and other magical peoples tended to gather around convergences, forming whole towns around the conduits that fed our magic. It was unusual that Alec's parents had purchased a place so far from a convergence. Five miles wasn't much to an ordinary person, but it was a lot when all of life's conveniences hinged upon access to magic.

"How far are we, exactly, from the Academy?" I asked. Alec dropped a dusty map book on my lap, and I winced as it jostled my bad ankle.

"Sorry," he said, sounding the opposite of sorry. "About a hundred miles." He pointed to a spot on the open page, which he must have found for me. "Here. This place is remote."

"Are your parents hermits?" I asked, flipping through the pages to try and find the Academy so I could orient myself.

"They liked their privacy," he replied, tone going a bit steely. I wondered if he maybe didn't get along with his folks. It would explain why he wasn't going to be missed for Christmas and why he spent all of his time at the Academy.

"They don't anymore?" I quipped, smiling up at him from the map. I wasn't happy about this situation, but I could be civil.

Alec's face was unchanged as he replied, "They're dead."

"Oh," I replied, feeling myself flush with embarrassment. "Oh, gods, I'm so sorry. I didn't know."

Alec waved away my apology, looking down as he absently stroked the white ferret, which had taken up residence on his lap. "It was a long time ago."

"Still," I said, biting my lip and feeling awkward. "I'm sorry."

"You don't have to look at me like that, Sage," Alec drawled, furrowing his brow at me again. "I don't need your pity."

"It's not pity," I said, feeling defensive again. Why couldn't this man just accept my apology like a normal person? "I'm just sorry for bringing it up, if it causes you pain."

"I'm fine," he replied darkly. I raised my brows at him, and he growled, "Stop that."

I sighed in defeat, turning back to the map to find a leyline that connected the cabin to my parents' house. It was quite a distance, traveling through five different convergences, but I could definitely get my note there.

"Okay," I said, more to myself than to Alec, who I was sure had already lost interest in my plight. "Here goes nothing."

I pictured the leyline route I wanted the paper plane to travel, drawing on wind from the nearest line beneath the earth. The plane swooped up, barely missing the fire as it was sucked up the chimney and away.

"There," I said, sitting back and releasing the magic back into the earth while willing the lines to carry my message correctly. The sole leyline under the cabin had dimmed somewhat. Alec was right; we'd need to choose carefully what magic to practice so we didn't burn it out. It could take days for the natural magic of the earth to recharge a leyline. "Hopefully, that works. And hopefully, the snow melts by Christmas Eve."

"I wouldn't count on it," Alec replied, watching me with a strange expression on his face. "I've been snowed in here for weeks before."

"Weeks?" I squeaked, the word coming out thin and panicky. "I can't be stuck here for weeks. I have a dissertation to defend. And I have to undo the damage you've done with Dr. Dvaran," I added, throwing the accusation back at him.

"You keep saying that," Alec said, frowning at me with academic interest. "Why exactly do you think I'm talking about you at all with Dr. D?"

"Because you hate me," I laughed, surprised that he would need me to spell it out for him.

Alec's frown intensified, and he seemed to shift a bit closer as he said, "I don't know what gave you that impression, Sage, but I don't hate you."

"Please," I scoffed, rolling my eyes. "Spare me the professional niceties, *Dr. Ashcroft*. You've been condescending and dismissive toward me since the moment I stepped foot in the lab three years ago."

"I'm condescending and dismissive toward everyone," Alec said with complete sincerity. "It's not personal."

"Why on earth would you act like that with complete strangers?" I asked, throwing up my hands in confusion. "Why not, I don't know, be polite and friendly?"

Alec scowled as if the idea had never occurred to him. "Alec," he said, standing to stoke the fire. He walked into the kitchen, leaving me on the sofa.

"What?" I asked, feeling utterly confused by his response.

"You called me Dr. Ashcroft," he replied, the sound of mugs clinking from his direction. I heard water pouring and twisted to look at him. "But at least as long as we're stuck here, it's Alec. Tea?"

Chapter 3

THREE DAYS UNTIL CHRISTMAS

"Is THIS YOU BEING polite and friendly?" I asked suspiciously, accepting the mug of tea. It had a painted pattern of snowflakes on the outside, and the whole thing felt entirely too festive for the company.

"This is me being *normal*," Alec said, sitting to drink his tea on the sofa next to me. "I'm actually a very nice person if you get to know me." He sipped his tea with his brows raised, then held out a hand to me expectantly. "I'm Alec. Nice to meet you."

I rolled my eyes, sipping the tea. It was something with orange and cinnamon, and it tasted like Christmas in a cup. "You don't need to patronize me."

"Is this *you* being polite and friendly?" he asked, his lips quirking up on one side as he lowered his hand.

"I've *been* polite and friendly," I corrected. I chose to ignore the way his cheek dimpled when he smiled. "It's you who's cold and distant."

Alec sighed, leaning his head back against the couch and looking pained. "It's easier to keep people at arm's length at work," he said, his eyes darting to mine before returning to the ceiling. "But I'm sorry if you perceived that as hatred."

I wasn't sure what to do with this apology, so I said nothing and took another sip of tea instead. Despite his protestations of innocence, I knew Alec had criticized my work to Dr. Dvaran. Casimir had no reason to lie to me, and I couldn't let my guard down because of a pair of broad shoulders, a sob story, and a portal gone awry.

I wondered what Casimir would think of me being stuck in a cabin with Alec over Christmas. It was clear that Cas was interested in me, but something about him just didn't do it for me. He was perfectly handsome and polite, but he seemed...I didn't really know. Too eager? A bit insincere in his flattery?

Still, I was grateful for the heads-up about Alec's meddling with my research. Maybe after the holidays I should give him a chance.

"Still not convinced?" Alec asked in a tone that told me he already knew the answer. He sighed, pulling my file open on his lap.

"Hey," I said, reaching to grab the file. Alec held it away from me, stretching his arm out so I would have to climb over him to retrieve it. "You're not permitted to look at those."

"According to you, I already have," he pointed out, flicking the file once in emphasis. "Or do you believe me all of a sudden?"

I pursed my lips, scowling fiercely. To my annoyance, Alec laughed.

It was a rich sound, and it occurred to me that I had never heard him make it before. In the three and a half years we had worked together in the portomancy lab, he had never been more than irascible and cold.

"Thought so," he said, dropping the file back on his lap and flipping open the cover. "I have no idea why you would trust *Dr. Flint's* word over mine since he's both an idiot and a snake, but tell me what *he* told you I found objectionable."

Alec spoke Casimir's professional name like it was something foul, and I frowned.

"The translations of the Celtic runes," I replied stonily, watching him over the top of my mug. "And what do you mean he's a snake?"

Alec gave me a look that best translated to, "oh, honey, you poor deluded thing," before turning back to my work. He flipped a page, his long fingers scanning as he read in silence. It made me more nervous than Dr. Dvaran's patient, expectant look when he was waiting for me to explain something to his satisfaction.

Binx meowed, and Alec shot him a scowl.

"On cursory inspection, your translations look good," he said, flipping a page and frowning at the file. "I'd have to read them in greater detail to know for sure, but I can promise you this is the first time I've seen these."

"They do?" I asked, shock at the praise rocking me to my foundations. "It is?"

"They do," he confirmed, closing the file and pinning me with a thoughtful expression. "And it is. I can think of at least one reason that Dr. Flint would lie to you about the quality of your work."

Max made a squeaking noise, and Alec rolled his eyes at the white ball of fur. "Fine, I'll find you something to eat, you bottomless pit of need. Does the cat need something, too?" he asked me, rising from the sofa as the ferret scrambled up his arm. "I'd hate for him to get peckish and eat my familiar."

"Probably," I said, still a bit stunned at his answer about Casimir and his praise. "Wait, what's the reason?"

"Later," Alec said, giving Binx a cautionary scratch on the head. To my intense surprise, the furry little traitor purred. "Food first. They're not the only hungry ones."

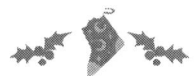

I felt more than a little useless, trapped on the couch with a busted ankle while Alec rummaged in the enchanted freezer for something edible.

"This might be meat," he said, a bit more skeptically than I would prefer for meat. I heard the plastic thwack of Tupperware being opened and the beeping of a microwave, and I tried to distract myself by looking around the cabin.

It was weathered and dusty but had a cozy, quaint charm. I could imagine a family spending winters here, with a Christmas tree in one corner and a blazing fire. There was a fur rug, which I hoped was an imitation, and several squashy armchairs as well as the sofa. There was a small dining table near the kitchen and another door that must lead to some kind of bedroom. I assumed there must be a bathroom, too, and I'd probably need to ask about one sooner or later.

"When did you last come up here?" I called back as Alec made kitcheny noises behind me. I sent a surreptitious gust of wind toward the mantle, and a small cloud of dust rose like an angry little tornado. "I'm guessing awhile?"

"Years," Alec shouted over the beeping of the microwave. I smelled something faintly meaty, and my stomach rumbled. It was still early for lunch, but portal travel was disorienting at the best of times.

Binx meowed hungrily, leaping down from my lap and sniffing hopefully in the direction of food. I heard a quiet, "Here you go, Binx. Please don't eat my ferret," and smiled a little at this very un-Alec side of Alec I was witnessing.

Maybe I had been too quick to judge. Although, three and a half years of icy indifference toward me wasn't exactly a winning way to gain my friendship.

"Here," Alec said, returning to the sofa and handing me a bowl decorated with little pine trees. "The microwave enchantments are still working, so it should be the perfect temperature."

I scooped some of the brown mush up with a spoon and sniffed warily. It smelled like stew, and it looked like stew, but I waited for Alec to take the first bite. Just in case.

"Not poison," he declared after eating a second spoonful. "Eat up, Sage."

"Who enchanted this place?" I asked, blowing on the stew out of habit but finding that it was, as Alec had said, the perfect temperature.

"My parents," Alec replied, eyes focused on his own bowl. "A long time ago."

"I'm sorry," I said again, feeling awkwardly uncertain about what to say. "We don't have to talk about it."

"I don't plan to," Alec replied, voice still a bit hollow and stony. He looked up, frowning at me. "That was me being cold and condescending, wasn't it?"

"Yup," I said, giving him a wry smile as I ate my stew. "Classic Dr. Ashcroft."

"I don't do it on purpose," Alec said, still frowning at me.

"I just bring it out in you, I suppose?" I teased, trying to coax that dimple back.

Alec didn't smile, looking concerned instead. "No, I just mean—" He paused, frown relaxing. "You're making fun of me."

"Just a bit," I agreed, taking another bite of stew. "This is pretty good. How long do you think it's been in that freezer?"

"Probably ten years," he replied, scraping the bowl loudly.

I choked on a wayward carrot, coughing inelegantly. "Ten years? That's some powerful enchanting."

He shrugged and held out a hand for my bowl. "My parents were powerful magic wielders," he said, placing both bowls on the coffee table in front of us. "I'm going to check the height of the snow drift, then make sure the generator won't give out on us. Will you be fine here?"

I gestured to the cozy room, now much warmer after the fire had been blazing for an hour. "Am I likely to be attacked in here? Is there a magical snow monster somewhere lurking in wait?"

"You're a smartass," Alec said, standing and stretching so that a sliver of tan stomach peeked out from beneath the flannel shirt. I pointedly refused to admire the firm skin and muscles I saw there, focusing on the wall behind him instead. "See if you can channel some healing magic into that ankle."

I rolled my eyes. I decided not to bother telling Alec that I had never managed a healing spell on anything larger than a papercut. Healing required a complex charm and some understanding of the human body, and I'd never had the patience to practice it. I could translate runic texts from five different obscure languages *and* create magical portals to almost anywhere in the world—and a few places *not* in this world—but healing a sprain was far beyond me.

I busied myself thinking about what reason Casimir would have to lie to me. He was a postdoc like Alec, so there wasn't any reason for him to envy my position or my mentorship under Dr. Dvaran. Faculty positions were highly competitive, but there was no way I'd get one right out of the PhD program. I'd likely end up doing several years of postdoc work like him and Alec before actually landing a research or tenure-track teaching role anywhere.

Alec must be mistaken. Maybe the whole thing had been a misunderstanding, and Dr. Dvaran hadn't wanted to see me urgently after all. He had left for India even though we had an appointment, so maybe it hadn't been all that important.

I sighed, thinking about my parents and sisters all at home wondering where I was. They would probably be making cookies or stuffing stockings with ridiculous charms, and I bet the house smelled like apples and cinnamon. An unexpected wave of home-sickness hit me, and the little cabin suddenly felt colder and more isolated. I had never missed a Christmas with my family, and I couldn't believe that a fluke portal accident would be the reason I missed this one.

Binx hopped back up onto the couch as I pulled out my phone again, still essentially a fancy brick without any network or wifi. I sighed, swiping through the photos my sisters had sent me when they arrived home two days ago, waiting for me to finish up my semester. They looked like me, caramel haired and blue-eyed, the grumpy cat and toad staring stoically at the camera as both women grinned.

Willow was two years older, and Paisley a year younger than me, and they fought endlessly when I wasn't home to act as a referee. Mom was probably already going out of her mind, and Dad would be hiding in the garage to "escape the estrogen."

"Generator still runs, which is a small mercy," Alec shouted, slamming the door that must lead to the garage. To my horror, I realized I had teared up, and I quickly brushed away the moisture that betrayed my emotion.

Alec froze when he saw me, frowning again. "What's wrong?"

"Nothing," I said, trying to sound innocent and raising my brows expectantly.

"You're crying," he argued flatly, picking up a box of tissues from a little side table and blowing off ten years of dust.

"I'm not," I protested, trying to smile.

It was unconvincing, and Alec thrust the tissue box at me awkwardly. "What's wrong?" he repeated.

"I'm fine," I insisted, taking a tissue despite myself. "It's just my ankle."

Alec still looked unconvinced, but he turned his attention to my ankle, where the ice pack was already thawing. "Did you try healing it?" he asked, crouching before the coffee table where it was resting. He lifted the ice pack and hissed at the purple swelling.

"I'm not very good at healing spells," I confessed, hating to admit any kind of weakness to the man my doctoral advisor once called his "most promising student ever."

"Of course you're not," he sighed, still looking at my ankle.

"What's that supposed to mean?" I asked indignantly, feeling emotion rise in me again and squashing it down. Clearly, the reality of my situation and the pain from the sprain was taking a toll, and I refused to cry in front of my arch-nemesis.

"Sage," he said, giving me a hard look. "Please stop assuming that everything I say is an insult. I only meant that the universe seems to be pushing us together for some reason because I happen to be *exceptional* at healing spells. I'm not trying to insult your abilities."

"Oh," I said, not sure how to respond to this. "Well, maybe work on your delivery a—what are you doing?" I asked. I hissed as he lifted my ankle and sat before me on the coffee table, resting my foot in his lap.

He gave me another frustrated look. "Trying to help you," he said, unlacing the boot, which was digging into the swelling something fierce. "This should have come off as soon as you realized you were hurt," he chastised, sighing as he pulled the laces and wiggled the boot off my foot.

I cried out, sharp pain shooting up my leg, and he stilled. "Sorry," he said, sounding genuinely apologetic. "That was hopefully the worst of it. Can you wiggle your toes?"

"I think so," I gritted out. I tried to wiggle my toes in my socks, which were covered in festive-colored cat paws.

He gave me a lopsided smile, the dimple making a momentary appearance. "Nice socks."

"I like cats," I said, a bit more defensively than necessary.

"I know," Alec laughed, gently testing the joint. "Just a sprain, I think. Give me a moment."

"How do you know how to heal sprained ankles?" I asked. I winced again as he gently prodded my ankle, closing his eyes in concentration as he felt around the swollen joint.

I hissed again, and he nodded as if he had discovered some key part of the injury. "Because I did my undergrad in medicine," he replied, surprising me. Alec seemed so wholly invested in portomancy that I never expected he would have studied anything else. "Now shhh."

I obeyed, tensing as Alec gently wrapped one hand around the sole of my foot. "Relax, Sage," he said, eyes still closed as if he were trying to visualize my foot.

"Sort of hard to do when your arch-nemesis has your injured ankle in his hands," I joked, trying to do as he bid and relax my leg.

"Arch-nemesis is a bit dramatic, don't you think?" he asked, a faint smile still ghosting his lips. He whispered something in what I thought might be ancient Greek, and the pain in my ankle began to ease.

I sighed audibly. I hadn't realized how much the damn thing hurt until Alec started to ease the pain. He murmured a few more words, touching different parts of my ankle as he worked, and by the time he was done, there was only a dull ache left beneath his gentle hands, the swelling considerably less and the bruising a muddy sort of yellow.

"Would your arch-nemesis do that?" he teased, opening his eyes to inspect his work. "You should be able to put weight on it now at least, but you should rest it if you can for another day."

"Thank you," I said, feeling very awkward that he was still holding my foot in his lap. "I doubt I'll be going anywhere, so that shouldn't be a problem."

"Good," he said, still holding my foot in his hands. I had never taken the time to really look at his hands, which were usually formed into specific shapes for manipulating portal magic. They were large and warm and firm, and my gut made a strange swooping sensation as I met his gaze, his eyes a dark brown in the dim light of the stormy afternoon.

"You can let go now," I pointed out, biting my lip uncertainly.

"Right," he said, giving himself a little shake. He squeezed my foot one last time as he placed it back on the coffee table and propped it up on a pillow. "Of course."

He scrubbed his hand through his hair, and the unruly, dark waves made my stomach lurch again.

Binx meowed loudly, startling us both out of our stupor.

"I'll go see if I can find anything to keep us busy," he said awkwardly, clearing his throat and giving me a sheepish smile.

I nodded, not trusting my mouth to say something that I wouldn't later regret.

Alec Ashcroft, my nemesis, had healed my ankle. Had made me lunch. Had fed my cat.

And I thought he had also perhaps given me butterflies.

Chapter 4

THREE DAYS UNTIL CHRISTMAS

THE AFTERNOON PASSED INTERMINABLY despite the diversions Alec attempted to produce. There was a battered copy of Clue—the board game, not the excellent Tim Curry movie—more books on portomancy than seemed normal in a vacation cabin that he claimed not to have visited in ten years, and a deck of cards with all of the jacks somehow missing.

He spent a while trying to get the TV to pick up a signal, giving up after an hour of listening to snowy static.

"Maybe there are some old DVDs around here," he sighed, looking irritably at Clue as if it were responsible for our current predicament.

"There's a lot to read, at least," I said, examining an ancient book on portomancy I had never heard of with the ponderous title of *Portale Magick and Other Such Craft.* "Why are there so many books on portomancy here?"

"They belonged to my parents," Alec replied absently, studying the stack with distaste. "They're wildly out of date, though. Mostly kept for posterity rather than for actual research."

"Your parents studied portomancy too?" I asked, looking up in surprise. There were many surprising things I was learning about Alec Ashcroft, I realized.

More alarmingly, I wanted to learn more.

"They're why I got into the field," he replied, refusing to elaborate more than the bare essentials as usual.

"After studying medicine," I said, considering his profile.

"Yes," he agreed, narrowing his eyes at me. "Why the third degree, all of a sudden?"

"We're stuck here," I replied with a shrug. "And I'm bored. Wait—why do you think Cas lied about Dr. Dvaran?" I asked, changing gears as I remembered he had never answered the question. "And why do you think he's a snake?"

Alec raised a brow at me in an attempt to hide his obvious relief that I had dropped the subject of his parents.

"To answer both of your questions, I have a *hypothesis*," he corrected. "Academics don't guess, Sage."

I threw an embroidered snowflake pillow at him. "You're being condescending again."

He grinned, catching the pillow and holding it in his lap as the dimples reappeared.

The fucking dimples. They shouldn't affect me as much as they did, but they softened him.

I would miss those dimples.

"My *hypothesis*," Alec continued, interrupting my traitorous thoughts, "is that Dr. Flint plans to steal your research and pass it off as his own."

"What?" I gaped, horror clenching in my gut. "He wouldn't do that! He could never get away with it, for starters."

"He's done it before," Alec said, looking stony. "His father is on the ethics review board and covered it up."

"What? How do you know he's done it before?" I asked, a sinking suspicion filling me with dread.

"Because it was my research he stole," Alec said unemotionally. "He was given a slap on the wrist, but I'd bet my familiar that he's not above doing it again."

"That's—" I cut myself off, trying to reorient in my new reality. "There are records of this?"

"There are," Alec verified, clearly unsurprised that I didn't believe him. "How much of your research has he seen? He's after a faculty position, and Dr. Dvaran would perhaps look past his youthful *indiscretion* if he were to present something truly outstanding."

"Oh gods," I blanched, panic overtaking me as the weight of this revelation settled on me. "He's seen all of it. He—" I swallowed, feeling vaguely sick. "He has a copy of some of my translations."

"Hey," Alec said, leaning toward me and taking my hands in his. "No one will steal your research, Sage. I'll make sure of it. We'll clear all of this up when we get back. I promise."

"*We*?" I asked, frowning at Alec's hands atop mine.

"We," he confirmed, squeezing once. A bolt of something flashed through me, the sincerity in his eyes making me truly believe that everything would be okay. "I'll make sure Dr. D knows the truth."

"Thank you," I said a bit shakily, squeezing Alec's hand in return. "I'm sorry he stole your work. I didn't know."

"Not your fault," Alec said, sighing as he dropped my hands and sat back. I felt unexpectedly cold at the loss of him. "But it boils my blood that he'd do it to you. Especially since—"

He cut himself off with a shake of his head, looking away.

"Since what?" I asked, daring to scoot closer to him.

He shrugged, looking slightly enraged. "I've seen how he looks at you."

"And how is that?" I asked, narrowing my eyes. I knew Casimir had been interested in me, and I was even more grateful that I had never taken him up on one of his offers for a date.

"Like he wants to get in your pants," Alec replied, a muscle in his jaw popping in irritation. "He's always staring at you. He's asked me to switch shifts with him multiple times when you were also expected in the lab. And you're gorgeous. The fact that it would irritate me would be an added bonus."

"I—what?" I stammered, eyes wide at my now-former arch-nemesis. "I have no idea which of those to unpack first. He asked to switch shifts?"

"Multiple times," Alec confirmed, standing to put away the abandoned copy of Clue. "It was a pleasure to refuse him. I actually pulled rank a few times to take the shifts *he* already had with you."

"Why?" I asked, watching him tidy away the game, his back rippling distractingly. "You hate me."

"We've already established that I don't, Sage," Alec said, sighing as he turned back to me. "But believe what you like. I've never trusted him, and I certainly don't trust him around *you*."

"So you think he wants to discredit me *and* sleep with me?" I asked, my voice a bit flatter than I intended.

Binx mewed, annoyed at the lack of attention I was paying him, and I shushed him with pets.

"He'd be a fool not to want to sleep with you," Alec replied, casting me a sideways glance. "For the reasons I already gave you."

"You think I'm gorgeous," I said, unable to keep a hint of teasing out of my tone.

"Empirically, yes," Alec said, sitting back and sweeping his gaze over me appraisingly. I felt myself flush under his gaze, his own rather heated. "Subjectively, I suppose it depends on the eye of the beholder."

"You're an ass," I said, glaring at him.

"Probably," he agreed, giving me a half smile as he pulled my feet into his lap and began to knead the soles. "Doesn't mean I'm wrong."

What the—? Alec Ashcroft was giving me a foot massage. And he thought I was empirically attractive.

"It probably doesn't help that Dr. D is planning to offer you the faculty position in the spring," Alec said, still massaging my feet.

"He's what?" I squealed. I sat up excitedly, almost digging my heel into Alec's groin as that little nugget of information suddenly registered. He huffed a laugh, shifting his hold on me so that I didn't castrate him accidentally. "How do you know?"

"Because he asked my opinion," Alec said, meeting my eyes as he dug his thumb into my foot. It felt amazing, and I almost moaned, the feeling unfamiliar and tingly and altogether too distracting.

"Stop that," I said, batting at his hands, which he grabbed at playfully in response, pulling me close so that our faces were only inches apart. "You can't be serious."

"I am," he replied, meeting my gaze steadily. "There are two faculty positions in the department next year, and Dr. Dvaran asked me who I'd offer them to. I told him me, obviously, and you."

"Obviously," I mocked, rolling my eyes. "But why me? I'm not a postdoc."

"You're a known entity," Alec said, smiling faintly as if this were a compliment. "And your work is solid. I'd rather work with you than someone new."

"Oh," I said, sitting back and frowning. Something deflated a bit in my chest. "So I'm just the lesser of two evils, then."

"Fuck, no," Alec growled, the curse surprising me. I rarely heard the stoic and cold Dr. Ashcroft swear.

It was kind of hot.

"Gods, I'm totally fucking this up," Alec sighed, dropping his head on the back of the couch and gesticulating at the ceiling. "Look, I'm trying to say that your work is sound, you're a brilliant witch, Casimir is a prick who doesn't deserve you, and Dr. Dvaran probably wanted to meet with you to gauge your interest in staying on with the department after graduating."

He sat back up, frowning at me as if he couldn't figure out what exactly he was doing.

"You'd be an asset, Sage," he said, cupping my chin gently, then clearly thinking better of it as he dropped his hand. "And I'll help however I can."

"You will?" I asked. Alec had called me brilliant. And gorgeous. And an asset. Something in my mind tilted on its axis, making my heart beat just a bit faster.

"Of course," he said, smiling in a way that seemed more resigned than actually pleased. "That's what friends do."

Friends. Alec and I were friends now, somehow.

That was fine. Everything was fine.

Except that I had a sinking feeling as he got up to forage for dinner in the enchanted freezer, his biceps visible through the flannel shirt as he fed Binx and Max and asked me about any food allergies, that I was maybe starting to want him to be more.

Oh, no.

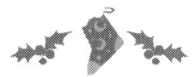

Alec insisted I take the bed, like the gentleman I was realizing he actually might be.

"The couch is fine," he insisted for the tenth time, pushing me through the bedroom door, my ankle still making me limp a little. "The pullout is busted, but it's comfy enough. Plus, you're injured."

"Barely," I argued, biting my lip anxiously. "Are you sure—"

"Go," he growled, pointing to the wooden, four-poster bed. It was dusty like everything else, but a quick gust of wind would take care of the worst of it. Flannel blankets and a big, thick comforter lay atop the bed. It looked eminently cozy surrounded by wooden walls and hand-stitched tapestries and glass domed lamps. "We can switch tomorrow, if you insist."

I agreed, mostly because the bed *did* look inviting, and I was feeling bone-tired from the small magics I'd been using all day to surreptitiously clear some of the dust and make the cabin habitable.

"Good night, Alec," I said finally, watching him retreat back to the living room.

He paused, turning and offering me a half-smile. "Good night, Sage."

Chapter 5

Two Days Until Christmas

WHEN I WOKE ON Christmas Eve Eve, it was to the sound of crashing and banging in the main room accompanied by wood splintering and masculine cursing. I groaned, rolling groggily out of the bed and hissing at the twinge of pain as I put my weight on my ankle. I was able to stand, which was a huge improvement, but it was stiff from sleep and still a little swollen.

The cursing intensified, so I shook myself more awake, pulling a blanket over my shoulders and scooping up Binx as I opened the bedroom door.

"What's going—OH!"

Alec looked up, his cheeks pink and dark hair dusted with snow, a moth-eaten snow jacket and worn-through gloves obviously not enough to ward off the cold. He smiled sheepishly, gesturing to a scraggly little tree that he had clearly been carrying a moment before.

He was surrounded by cardboard boxes that looked like they'd been buried under dust for a decade—which they probably had. The sparkling ends of tinsel stuck tantalizingly out of the top of several boxes.

"Since we might be stuck here for Christmas," he said, his tone hesitant as he rubbed the back of his neck and turned even more pink, "I found a tree. And I pulled all of the old ornaments and decorations from storage. I figured you might want to decorate."

On his shoulder, the ferret chirped happily, and Binx mewed in approval.

"I—" I must have looked like a strange, alien fish, opening and closing my mouth repeatedly in shock.

Binx meowed again more loudly, reminding me that humans speak.

Alec grinned, the dimple appearing. "That's what I thought. There's toast and hot cocoa in the kitchen."

Alec Ashcroft, the resident grinch and generally unlikeable ass at the Academy, wanted to decorate for Christmas. He made hot cocoa and dragged in a tree, and he blushed and dimpled now.

Maybe that portal had taken us to a whole other dimension without me realizing it.

I wrapped the blanket tighter around me, eating toast and drinking cocoa in stunned silence as I watched Alec put up the tree and sort box after box of dusty ornaments and garlands, placing items in organized piles on the coffee table.

"My family used to do this every Christmas," he shared, gesturing to the boxes by way of explanation. "I—" He cut himself off with a grimace. "I normally wouldn't, but since you're stuck here..." He trailed off, looking at me like an academic puzzle he was hoping to crack.

I beamed. "Gods, yes, I want to decorate for Christmas!" I said, placing the snowman mug in the sink and almost skipping to the ornaments. "Do you have a star or an angel? My family does a star because, duh, pagans, but I know..."

I trailed off when I looked up and saw his face, a mixture of tentative joy and obvious devastation.

"What's wrong?" I asked, standing and wobbling a bit on my bad ankle. He caught me, guiding me to the couch. "Alec?"

"I just..." he shook his head, taking a steadying breath as Max moved from his shoulder to curl around his neck protectively. "I lost my parents during the holidays. It's why..."

He didn't need to finish the thought. It was why he didn't celebrate. Why he stayed at the university and kept himself cold and distant. Why the cabin and the ornaments all looked like they hadn't been touched in a decade.

"I'm so sorry," I said, cringing at the apology as I put a tentative hand on Alec's knee. He probably didn't want my pity, but he surprised me. He covered my hand with his own, and a little spark of something warm buzzed up my arm. Magic was a strange beast. I took a breath before continuing. "We don't have to—"

"It's why I switched to portomancy." He looked up finally, his jaw set determinedly in a very Alec sort of expression. "From medicine. I'm interested in it, obviously, but mostly it was a way to feel connected to them."

"Gods," I whispered, feeling my heart break for him as I gently squeezed his knee. "We don't have to decorate, Alec."

"It's fine," he said, standing as the mask of the chilly Dr. Ashcroft slid over his face. "I'm sorry. I shouldn't have—"

He grimaced again, cursing softly as he stood. "I'm going to start melting a path to the nearest convergence point," he said, stepping away from me. "You decorate. I know you miss your family. Perhaps we can get you home by Christmas."

He walked out without another word or backward glance, Max whining a little around his neck.

Maybe Alec was becoming a puzzle *I* needed to crack. This hot and cold thing was getting very confusing.

I looked at the boxes of ornaments—ten years of joy and memories hidden away as Alec threw himself into his work—and felt wretched that I'd complained about missing my family.

Alec had no warm Christmas cauldron brew, or tree decorating traditions, or siblings squabbling over the last gingerbread cookie. No wonder he was cold and standoffish in the lab.

Although, he thought I was brilliant. And gorgeous. And he had refused to switch shifts with Casimir. With the way he had been looking at me since arriving at the cabin, I had begun to suspect that he had more of a reason than just not trusting our colleague.

And this Christmas, he was not alone.

I put Binx down, ignoring his meow of protest as I rolled up my sleeves.

It was time to make some magic.

Chapter 6

TWO DAYS UNTIL CHRISTMAS

ALEC WAS OUTSIDE MOST of the day, returning only briefly to use the bathroom and staunchly ignoring anything I was doing.

It was just as well, because by the time the sun was setting, the cabin gleamed and sparkled like Christmas had come early.

I used every ornament in every box, hanging garlands and tinsel and stockings and holly until every corner of the cabin was joyful and warm and welcoming.

I found out that Alec's parents had preferred a star atop their tree, like mine, and that they had saved every handprint ornament he had ever made them. It hurt my heart a little, both seeing tiny Alec grow up, and knowing that his parents had missed so much of his life.

Some decorations were enchanted, the charms old and weakening, but still active. A red train set chuffed merrily around the base of the tree, which I had fluffed the best I could without magic, and several ornaments spun in place or twinkled brightly of their own accord. There were stockings that looked to be hand-knitted, with little snowflakes and pine trees and Santa hats dancing merrily around the cuffs, and several spools of garland made my job much easier by twining themselves around columns and the beams of the roof.

"Dear gods, it's like Christmas threw up in here," Alec said behind me, causing me to spin.

A freshly baked tray of gingerbread cookies still steamed in my oven-mitted hands, and I had donned an old Christmas apron and a pair of jingling antlers to feel festive.

Alec burst into laughter. "What in the hells are you doing?" he asked. He grinned as he flicked a jingling antler atop my head.

He looked exhausted, probably drained from using magic and drawing on an increasingly weak leyline all day.

I beamed, pleased that he at least wasn't upset. I had been worried that being assaulted by Christmas might make him shut down and shut me out, but maybe a day freezing in the snow had made him more inclined to warmth and cheer.

"Baking cookies," I replied, nodding to the tray of misshapen gingerbread lumps. "They were supposed to be gingerbread men, but I think I made them too runny. I had to get a bit creative with ingredients."

"Do I want to know what's in them?" he asked, removing a damp glove and gingerly picking up a hot cookie. What should have been the head broke off into his mouth, and he fumbled the cookie. "It's hot."

"Of course, it's hot," I said, rolling my eyes. "They just came out of the oven. I thought you were an intelligent academic."

I placed the cookies on the counter, smiling when I heard another snap of gingerbread from behind me.

"Pretty good," Alec declared through a mouthful of cookie. "I didn't know you could bake."

"I'm full of hidden talents," I said, realizing belatedly that it sounded rather suggestive when trapped in an isolated cabin together. Alec raised an eyebrow, and I blushed, speaking rapidly to hide my embarrassment. "You'd better take off your coat. You're dripping all over the floor. How did the snow clearing go?"

"Slowly," Alec replied, shaking off the coat and depositing ice and snow all over the kitchen floor. I sighed. Men. He grinned, letting a tongue of fire lick over the stones and evaporate the water. "So persnickety."

"It's *your* house," I pointed out, removing the apron and baking mitts and placing them on the counter. "I'm trying to be courteous."

"Yes, I can see that," Alec said, admiring the festival chaos with a whistle. "Christmas has exploded."

"Is it too much?" I asked, feeling a bit crestfallen. Of course, this wasn't his thing. He hadn't done Christmas in ten years, and here I was, trying to shove it down his throat. "I can take it down."

"Hey," he said, catching my hand as I turned toward the mantle. "No. Don't, Sage. It's magic. You made magic."

I met his gaze, his tentative smile drawing one of my own. "Well, I *am* almost a doctor of portomancy," I joked, vaguely aware that he was still holding my hand.

"You are," Alec agreed, smiling properly and squeezing my hand. "And *you're* magical, Sage."

I flushed, feeling my cheeks burn and something fluttering excitedly in my chest. Lower.

"Magical, empirically gorgeous, an asset," I joked, trying to ease the sudden explosion of emotion I felt as everything went tight and hot and loose in me all at the same time. "I suppose you can't be my arch-nemesis anymore."

"I hope not," Alec replied, his gaze steady as his brown eyes met my blue ones. He squeezed my hand again before dropping it, making a show of inspecting the tree and the stockings and the enchanted ornaments.

I used the time to give myself a stern talking-to. Alec was my *colleague*. My recently-former-arch-nemesis. I could *not* be having butterflies for or around him.

"I'd forgotten about these," Alec said, blessedly distracting me from my line of thought as he examined the stockings on the mantle. "My mother made them. Mine was the one with the Santa hats."

"She made them?" I asked, joining him by the toasty fire. I held out a hand to touch the Santa hat stocking. The neat pattern was knitted precisely but with enough variation to be able to tell it was handmade. "She was very talented."

"She was," Alec agreed, his voice edged with sadness again.

I looked up to see his eyes lined with silver, and cleared my throat awkwardly. "Tell me about your research."

Work was an excellent topic of distraction, it turned out, and three hours later, the fire burned low as several empty mugs of cocoa sat between us.

"Once I've mapped the convergences that overlap our own, I can move between universes," Alec said, gesturing in the air as if he could show me what he meant. "I just need to figure out the tethering issue."

"You'd need an anchor back to this plane," I said thoughtfully, my mind happily occupied with magical theory as we batted ideas back and forth for how such a journey might be accomplished without Alec being lost to nothingness. "Perhaps the connection to your familiar?"

I gestured to Max, who was asleep in Alec's breast pocket, his furry white tail poking out like a strangely long paintbrush.

Alec sighed, looking into the fire. "Perhaps," he agreed. "But I'm not sure if I'd be willing to risk it."

I stroked Binx absently in my lap, and he purred contentedly as silence stretched between us. The crackling fire and purring cat and sounds of the wind outside were a soothing lullaby. I stifled a yawn, finding myself unwilling to go to bed just yet.

"Why Max?" I asked, nodding to the ferret in Alec's pocket. He turned to me, raising a brow in question. "Why name him that?"

"You won't believe me if I tell you," Alec said, smiling as I raised my own eyebrows.

"Try me," I said, stroking Binx's head. "I named mine after a movie cat, after all."

"That's the thing," Alec said, leaning back on the sofa, his arms spread wide over the back, and his eyes fixed on me. "I named him after the kid in Hocus Pocus."

"You did not," I laughed, incredulous that I had forgotten the main character of my favorite Halloween movie was called Max. To be fair, the Sanderson sisters totally stole the show, but still. "You're just saying that because of Binx."

"Nope," Alec said, shaking his head and reaching up to tug gently on a loose lock of my hair. The gesture felt strangely intimate, and I didn't hate it. "Hocus Pocus is perhaps the greatest cinematic masterpiece of all time."

"Now you're teasing me," I accused, smiling as I stood to clear away the mugs.

"Maybe," Alec conceded, grinning as he stood to help. "But it really is my favorite movie."

"Mine too! Look at us, finding things in common," I joked, turning from the sink to find Alec right behind me, his broad chest inches away from mine. I swallowed, feeling suddenly flushed. "Perhaps this was a plot by Dr. Dvaran to force us to get along."

"Perhaps," Alec agreed, his eyes darkening as he flicked his eyes to my lips. I felt a tug of desire, a feeling echoed in the hungry gaze in his eyes.

Gods, it had been a long time since I'd felt something like that toward anyone. If I'd told myself three days ago that I'd be feeling it for *Alec*, I'd have locked myself up and thrown away the key.

Something small and round fell from the ceiling and hit me in the head.

"What the—?" We both looked up at the same time, and Alec cursed softly under his breath as I laughed. "Mistletoe."

"This damn cabin always was a meddlesome busybody," Alec growled, shooting an accusing glare at the ceiling. The mistletoe twitched, and another white berry fell, this time hitting Alec in the face.

I laughed again. "It certainly seems to have opinions of its own, now that we've woken it up," I agreed, the cabin's behavior reminding me a bit of the Academy.

I plucked the berry from his collar where it had landed so that Max wouldn't try to eat it, looking up to find Alec gazing at me intently. My stomach did another flip, some conflict warring behind his eyes.

"It's late," he said, moving imperceptibly closer. "You should go to bed."

"You too," I agreed, my body seeming to lean toward his like he was the portal into which I was inexorably falling.

Something like indecision flashed across his face before he sighed, frowning as he leaned forward and kissed my forehead.

"Good night, Sage," he said, stepping back far enough that it was clear he meant this as my cue to leave.

I felt warm shivers travel down my spine from the spot where he kissed me, mixed with confusion. Had I misread him? I thought he'd been interested, but clearly he wasn't totally sure what he wanted.

I sighed, scooping up Binx and replying in a hushed voice, "Good night."

Chapter 7

ONE DAY UNTIL CHRISTMAS

IT WAS STILL DARK out when I awoke to the sound of someone shouting, crying out as if in fear or agony. I couldn't really be sure.

I rolled out of bed, disoriented but finally able to stand properly without any twinge of pain in my ankle, and threw open the bedroom door, grabbing a blanket to cover me.

I was still wearing my sensible sweater—thank goodness the cabin had a working washing machine—but I couldn't sleep in slacks, and I didn't particularly want the Christmas-themed granny panties I had worn with this outfit on full display.

Alec was sitting up, his form silhouetted by the dim fire in the hearth as he panted, sweat gleaming on his bare back as I approached.

"Alec," I said, speaking from far enough away that I hoped I wouldn't startle him. "Are you alright?"

"Go back to sleep, Sage," he replied, his voice dark and cold and nothing like it had been earlier when we had bounced ideas about portal tethering back and forth.

"What's wrong?" I asked, ignoring his command and moving around the sofa to sit next to him.

I blushed, now realizing he was wearing only his boxer briefs to sleep, his tan, muscular legs bent as he sat with his elbows on his knees and his dark head bowed.

The image was a sharp contrast to the joyful twinkling lights and ornaments around him, and I put a tentative hand on his shoulder.

He didn't bat it away, which I felt was a good sign.

"Did you have a nightmare?" I asked, feeling his shoulder tremble slightly beneath my hand. "Your parents?"

"Yes," he murmured, not looking up or moving as he stared at the ground.

"I'm sorry," I said gently. "I shouldn't have done all of this. I didn't mean—"

"Stop apologizing for things that aren't your fault," Alec said, his voice cold and harsh. "This isn't about you."

"I know that," I said, trying not to sound defensive. "I'm sor—fine, I'm *not* sorry. But I want to help."

"You can't," he said, sounding so adamant that I almost convinced myself to believe him.

Binx meowed, demanding cuddles, and I scooped him up, placing him next to me on the couch.

Gently, I lifted my hands to cup Alec's cheeks, his face still glaring purposefully at the floor as if he could will a portal into existence beneath his feet.

"You don't have to be alone, Alec," I said, trying to keep my tone soothing but honest. "Not at the holidays, and not in your grief. You can let people in. You can let *me* in."

Alec sighed, shaking his head.

Outside the windows, the snow continued to fall, the moon still high in the sky. It was the middle of the night, and Alec had been clearing snow all day, expending the gods knew how much magic.

He needed sleep.

When Paisley had been little, she'd suffered from night terrors so awful that only our mom holding her through the night could get her back to sleep following an episode.

Not entirely sure that what I was doing was a good idea, but feeling simultaneously like it was the best idea I had ever had, I climbed into Alec's lap, straddling him so we were face to face.

He gaped, looking thunderstruck and a little panicked, putting his large hands around my hips to steady me more out of instinct than anything else.

"Lie down," I commanded, stroking my fingers soothingly through his hair. "I'll stay with you."

"Sage," he rasped, studying my face as if trying to decide if I was serious. "This is a bad idea."

"Some of the best discoveries come from bad ideas," I pointed out, running my fingers over his scalp again until he closed his eyes, his shoulders relaxing a fraction. "Now lie down."

He complied, pulling me down into the sofa with him as I wrapped my stolen blanket around us. It was warm with the fire so close, and Alec's body was like a furnace, hard and hot against mine as I pressed myself into his chest, winding my arms around him.

His arms came up to wrap around my back, and I pressed my cheek to his chest.

"You're safe," I said, repeating the words my mother had told Paisley whenever terrors dragged her from sleep. "You are not alone."

Alec's heart beat wildly in his chest, pounding so hard I could feel the rhythm of it against my cheek. My own heart felt uncontrollably fast, but I didn't move, staying wrapped up with him until his breathing and frantic pulse slowed, and I felt him relax into the embrace.

"Am I still your arch-nemesis?" he asked, his lips brushing my skin as he spoke against my temple. "Cold, imperious Dr. Ashcroft?"

"No," I said, nestling closer and reveling in the warmth of his skin against mine. "Right now, you're just Alec."

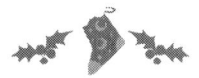

I had made a huge mistake.

Not totally unexpected in the wilds of academic research, but still a monumentally huge mistake.

I'd fallen asleep while holding and being held by my recently-former-arch-nemesis, and now sunlight was streaming through the window, and Alec was as hard as granite.

This was normal, I told myself, trying to decide whether or not to shift away. Men often had reactions like this in the morning. It had nothing to do with me or my proximity, or the fact that we had fallen asleep together on the couch with him barely clothed.

It also had nothing to do with the fact that he said I was gorgeous and brilliant, and that last night he had told me I was magic.

"Sage," came a gruff, not quite awake voice from above me. I felt Alec's arms tighten around me, his body shifting against mine as certain parts pressed closer, his face buried in my hair. "You smell like cookies and cinnamon."

"Not a bad thing on Christmas Eve," I quipped, deciding to give into the temptation to sink into him.

It had been a *long* time since I'd been with anyone, and Alec was solid and warm and smelled like pine trees and this dusty, old cabin. I felt my blood heat unbidden as his hand moved from my back to my hip. The warm wool blanket cocooned us from the morning cold, and it felt strangely like we were in a moment suspended in time, in a world all our own.

There would undoubtedly be consequences for this, but I was finding it very hard to care about them.

"I'm sorry," he murmured, still speaking against my temple as his nose brushed against my face. "For the nightmare. I didn't mean to wake you."

"Didn't you tell me last night to stop apologizing for things that aren't my fault?" I teased. I nuzzled against his chest, letting myself pretend that this was how it would always be. That this hadn't all been some ridiculous accident.

His arms tightened around me, and I had to stifle a gasp at the hard press of him against my stomach.

He stilled, loosening his arms.

"Gods, Sage, I—"

"Don't," I whispered, wriggling closer as he tried to let me go. "I'm cold."

The lie worked, and his arms tightened again as he drew me closer, throwing a bare leg over mine to pin me next to him.

"This is a dream, right?" he murmured, softening his body again until we were pressed together, all of his hard edges against my soft ones. "I'm dreaming."

"Do you often dream about waking up with your arch-nemesis in your arms?" I teased, feeling my stomach twist with a mixture of nervous excitement and desire as he seemed to grow somehow harder against me.

"I dream of waking up with *you* in my arms," he breathed, so quietly I would have missed it if we hadn't been flush against each other. He pressed again, groaning as he buried his face in the crook of my neck. "This can't be real."

"Alec," I breathed, my heart thumping furiously behind my chest as he drew me in and made warmth pool between my thighs. "What are we doing?"

"Feeling," he replied, letting me go suddenly and twisting me in his arms so my back was flush against his chest, his arms wrapped around my waist as his palms splayed flat against my sweater.

He pressed into me, his length hard against my backside. It made my nipples peak beneath the bra I still wore, everything feeling suddenly heavy and aching.

His fingers trailed to the hem, finding bare skin where the sweater rode up over my stomach, and I gasped, covering his hands with mine.

"Let me feel you," he begged, moving one hand up under my sweater as the other ventured lower. "Gods, Sage, I've wanted to touch you so badly for so long."

He stilled, holding me taut as a bowstring as I practically vibrated beneath his hands, my pulse a thrumming beat as he held me.

"What are you waiting for?" I asked, my voice pitched low and breathy in a way I'd almost never heard it.

"Permission," he murmured, pressing a kiss to my neck just under my ear.

Oh gods, were we doing this? Was I about to let my colleague and academic rival feel me up and dry-hump my backside on Christmas Eve morning?

Damned straight, I was.

Chapter 8

ONE DAY UNTIL CHRISTMAS

"FEEL ME," I SAID, relaxing my grip on his wandering hands and letting myself give in to sensation. To feeling.

How many times had I imagined Alec's competent hands, usually curved in casting runes or cramped around a pen, do exactly this?

Pre-cabin Sage would adamantly insist it was never.

But I had to admit to myself that it was more times than I had realized as one of his hands brushed the underside of my breast, the other finding the hem of my panties.

"You have no idea how often I have imagined this," Alec groaned, one finger sliding beneath the waistband of my panties to brush the curls beneath. His other hand shifted between us, fumbling with the clasp of my bra.

He cursed, and I let out an involuntary laugh, the tension of the moment too much for me. "Do you need help?"

"I have two gods-damned degrees and a PhD," he growled, finally releasing the clasp and moving his hand to cup my bare breast. I gasped, and he pressed hard against me again in satisfaction. "I can manage a fucking bra."

"Alec," I gasped as his fingers grazed my nipple and pinched gently. "How often?"

"What?" he asked, wholly distracted by the hand that was moving inexorably south. Any second, he would feel the evidence of how hot this was making me.

"How often have you imagined this?" I asked. I felt heat flood me in tingling waves as his fingers slid lower.

He brushed my arousal, and groaned again behind me. "Almost daily for three-and-a-half years," he breathed, sliding two fingers down as he pinched my nipple again. "Gods, Sage. You're so fucking wet for me."

"I know," I breathed, the flame of embarrassment dying as he kissed my neck, pressing his length hard against my backside. "And you're hard for me."

"Damn right, I am," he growled, thrusting gently against me as he slid his fingers down, down, down until they were parting me, teasing the sensitive bud between my thighs and making me gasp and squirm. "I told you. You're gorgeous and brilliant. I'd be a fucking fool to not want you."

"You never let on," I gasped, finding it hard to maintain the beat of the conversation as his fingers began working some magic I really wanted to learn to harness. The hand at my breast rolled and kneaded, making the other breast feel lonely and cold. I released his hands, using one to tease my other breast and reaching the other back to grip his hip behind me.

A moan escaped me, and I really hoped Binx and Max had made themselves scarce because they were about to be thoroughly traumatized if not.

"I couldn't when I was sure you hated me," he said, nipping at my earlobe with his teeth as he writhed against me, seeking his own pleasure as he worked on mine. "But the number of times I imagined bending you over one of the lab tables and taking you from behind..." He growled in approval as I shuddered and bucked against his hand, release shimmering just off in the distance. "Gods, I wanted to strangle Casimir every time he looked at you."

"No death threats," I breathed, trying to let myself become the feelings he was wringing from me as his fingers teased and circled and pinched. I thrust my hips, seeking friction and fullness. "Only this."

"Only this," he agreed with a soft chuckle as his fingers slipped lower, finding my entrance. "Stop me any time."

"I won't stop you," I said, writhing against his hand as I tried to force his fingers to where I wanted them. "Please, Alec."

He groaned at my begging, slipping his fingers into me as I ground against his hand, his lips on my neck as he watched me coming unraveled over my shoulder.

"That's it," he murmured as spasms began to wrack my body. "Come for me."

As if by some sensual magic, his words undid me, and I shuddered against him as pleasure shot down my spine from the top of my head to the tips of my toes, which curled under the blankets.

"Alec." I breathed his name like a prayer as I rode the waves of pleasure until they spiraled out into nothingness, feeling myself still abuzz with his hands in my most intimate places.

"That was—" He swallowed, interrupting himself as his hands shifted slightly, both moving away from where I wished they would stay, but not too far. "Fucking gods, please tell me we can do that again."

I laughed, turning in his arms to face him again, feeling my cheeks pink and flushed with pleasure and a twinge of self-consciousness. "What about you?" I ran my hands over his firm chest, feeling his length still pressed hard against my thigh. I moved my hands lower, teasing the ridges of muscle over his abdomen. "You should have a turn."

"You're right," he said, smirking in his usual self-assured way that no longer seemed completely arrogant.

He scooped me up unexpectedly, and I yelped in surprise as he carried me toward the bathroom.

It was the work of a moment to get undressed, both of us standing under the steamy water within minutes of Alec carrying me from the couch.

He looked down, examining every inch of my naked body in a way that made me feel oddly exposed but also powerful.

"Gods," he rasped, skating his hands reverently from my shoulders down my arms, over my breasts, and lower to brace my hips. He stepped closer, reaching back to cup my backside as he pulled my body flush against his. "I was an idiot to wait so long to make a move on you."

I laughed, beginning my own exploration of his body with my hands. The hard muscles of his chest and arms tapered to a narrow waist, and a perfect vee pointed to where I planned to end this shower.

"What about your two degrees and a PhD?" I teased, tracing the vee lower. He caught my hands, and I looked up, my hopefully seductive smile faltering in his serious gaze. "What's wrong?"

"I don't want you to do this because you feel obligated," he said, his voice gentle as his eyes bored into mine. "Until yesterday, you didn't even like me, and—"

I interrupted his speech with a kiss, soft and barely there, as I brushed my lips against his. It was the first time we had actually kissed, I realized, and I pulled back to look at him.

He looked rather like a deer in headlights.

"Until yesterday, I didn't really know you," I said, pressing a second gentle kiss to his lips. "Now that I do, I like you quite a lot. And I *want* to do this. Unless you don't?"

Alec's arm wound around my back as his hand threaded into my hair, and he pulled me in for a third kiss, deepening the movement as he held me tight against him and swept his tongue into my mouth.

This kiss was no gentle hesitation or experimental touch. It was consuming and branding, intense in the same way Alec was intense; focused and driven like he was trying to untangle a particularly stubborn magic.

I pulled back a little breathless, feeling him hard against me, his cock rigid at attention.

"I definitely do," he said, nipping at my bottom lip as if he didn't want to be parted from me for even a second. "Clearly, I'll have to provide you with additional evidence of my interest."

"Me first," I insisted, dropping to my knees before he could clutch me to him, running my hands down his hard, wet body as I knelt before him.

"Definitely dreaming," Alec hissed, fisting one hand in my hair and pressing the other against the cold tile of the shower as I touched him, licking him from base to tip. "Fucking gods."

I licked up the little bead of moisture that had gathered at his head, closing my mouth around him and sucking gently as I closed my hand around his base.

"Fuck," he groaned, his hand flexing in my hair as I sucked.

"You have a dirty mouth, Dr. Ashcroft," I teased, pulling back just long enough to speak before I took him fully in my mouth.

"You too," he growled, watching me like what I was doing was the hottest thing he had ever seen in his life. The pressure of his hand against my scalp urged me to move faster, and I explored with one hand while keeping the other firmly at his base. I cupped his balls, and he groaned. "Fuck, Sage."

"Later," I said, resuming my rhythm as we found one that worked for both of us. He began thrusting his hips, clearly holding back so that he didn't make me gag, which I appreciated. I responded by taking him as deeply as I could, putting gentle pressure around his base and his balls, and I worked my tongue over the delicate underside of his cock.

"Fuck," he shouted, his release filling my mouth so unexpectedly that he slipped out, spurting over my chest and breasts, and he held himself steady. "Fuck, I'm sorry."

He leaned his forehead against the cool tile, his body quaking as I pressed a kiss to his thigh and stood, letting myself be caged by his arms under the warm water. It washed away the evidence of what we had done, and I lifted my hands to cup his face.

"Don't," I whispered, kissing him gently as I coaxed his head off the wall and wrapped my arms loosely around his neck. "I have no complaints. The swearing *really* does it for me, by the way."

He huffed a laugh, pressing his lips to mine in a quick but thorough kiss. "I need a few hours," he breathed, his hands stroking my face and my hair, the water running over us in rivulets under the shower. "But I intend to have all of you later, Sage. I want to make every fucking inch of you mine, if you'll let me."

My toes curled, despite already being thoroughly sated this morning. He wrapped me in one last bruising kiss before grabbing the soap and lathering it, rubbing bubbles over both of us. His caress lit another fire within me, and I was abuzz once again as he shut off the water and reached for a fluffy towel.

"Long enough yet?" I asked, feeling a little disappointed when he laughed and pressed a kiss to my temple. He wrapped the towel around me first, reaching for a second to wrap around his waist.

"If only," he murmured, looking somewhat chagrined. "Magic can't do everything, unfortunately."

"Can you use magic for...*that*?" I asked, feeling myself blush, which was frankly ridiculous after what we had just done.

Alec laughed again, seeming happier and lighter than I had seen in the three and a half years of knowing him.

"None specifically," he replied, pulling me close again, the towel forcing me to behave. "But I'm not opposed to experimenting. I've heard that shadows can be *very* effective."

"Gods," I said, swallowing as I imagined myself pinned by shadow magic, then shook my head to clear the image.

Alec grinned. "Breakfast first," he said, grabbing my sweater and bra and ruined panties from the floor, along with his briefs. "And laundry. And I want to work on the snow pack again."

"So responsible," I sighed. I heard Binx meowing angrily outside the bathroom and realized that he hadn't had breakfast either. "I suppose we should take care of chores before playing, anyway."

"Hmm," Alec replied, kissing me soundly once more until I was breathless. He looked down at me, his eyes full of desire and mischief and intensity, gazing at me like he was studying at a particularly promising portal. "I intend to make *plenty* of time to play with you, Sage. Enough to make up for all of the times I didn't."

Chapter 9

ONE DAY UNTIL CHRISTMAS

THE REST OF THE day was filled with surreptitious caresses and longing looks and growing unfulfilled desire as we went about various chores, every second of the day leading to what I intended to be an explosive evening of lovemaking.

I made breakfast while Alec did a load of laundry, presenting me with clean panties as if they were a prize and suggesting that they might not survive the evening anyway.

We worked on clearing some of the snow through the afternoon, using fire magic from the leyline to melt the snow in a path toward the village. Binx and Max refused to join us, curling up in front of the fire as if they hadn't been ready to eat each other only a day before.

Another foot of snow had fallen overnight, but it was a more manageable depth than the ten feet or so that was packed around the rest of the cabin.

It was slow going and ineffective. By the time the sun had begun its descent, we had only melted about a mile between us and the nearest convergence.

Our work had been punctuated by a fierce snowball fight and a hot and heavy make-out session in part of the snowdrift that left me cold and shivering while flooded with heat at the same time. It had taken a great deal of willpower—and Alec refusing to do anything else with me until we had cleared several more feet—to force myself to focus.

To be fair, my motivation to clear the snow had lessened considerably, and Alec seemed to feel the same. Of course I wanted to see my family, but being trapped for a few days with an attractive wizard who was similarly invested in my pleasure was not a terrible alternative to my usual Christmas.

"We should eat something," Alec suggested, his arm around my shoulders as we trudged back to the cabin. Snow had seeped into every part of my boots and coat, borrowed from the moldering pile Alec had found in a closet, and I was a little worried that I couldn't feel my toes anymore.

It was still the best day of my life.

"More mystery meat?" I suggested, smiling up at him in the dying light. His cheeks and nose were adorably pink, and his dark hair was covered by a knitted hat with a ludicrously huge pom-pom on top and a pattern of little bears around the circumference.

"And gingerbread cookies," Alec reminded me, smiling down as if this were how things always were between us. Warm and friendly and open, no rivalry or barbed words or misunderstandings.

It made my stomach sink.

"What's wrong?" he asked, frowning as if my emotions were written plainly on my face.

"It's just..." I sighed, deciding that now was not the time to begin telling half-truths. "When we go back, will it still be like this?"

"What do you mean?" Alec asked, pausing in the entryway to stamp the snow from his boots as I did the same.

We climbed out of our snow gear while I tried to think of how to phrase my question, my heart hammering with uncertainty.

"Sage," he pushed, cupping my cheeks once his hands were free of their sodden gloves. His fingers were ice cold, and I shivered as he lifted my face to meet his questioning gaze. "Tell me."

"When we're back at the Academy," I explained, "and you're a postdoc, and I'm a grad student again, will it still be like this? Is this because of the cabin and Christmas, or is it real?"

"Real?" Alec frowned, stroking his cold thumbs over my cheekbones. "You're the most real thing in the world to me, Sage. And I intend to make sure everyone knows it."

He bent to kiss me, warming my lips with his as something like relief cracked in my chest. "It's not just Christmas magic clouding your judgment?" I whispered, putting words to the fear that had begun to plant roots in my gut.

Alec laughed, kissing me again soundly. "I'm a grinch, remember?" he teased, eyes twinkling a little in the lights of the tree. "Christmas has nothing to do with it."

"You weren't supposed to hear that," I winced, cursing myself for not expressing my opinions about his hatred of the holidays more quietly. Now that I knew the truth, it was no wonder that Alec didn't celebrate.

"But I think Christmas may be growing on me," he added, his gaze softening on mine as he smiled down at me. "As long as I get to spend it with you."

Dinner fell to the back burner as he kissed me, and I kissed him back fiercely while trying to maneuver us to the bedroom without letting him go.

He lifted me, and I wrapped my legs around him like an oversized octopus, wishing I had even more limbs to wrap around him.

He laughed, taking long, purposeful strides past the living room and kitchen and into the bedroom I'd been sleeping in.

I was ready to begin tearing his clothes from him, but rather than throwing me on the bed and ravishing me like I wanted, he put me down gently, holding my hands still while I tried to grasp at him.

"What are you doing?" I panted, trying to squirm my way out of his grip. He laughed again, pulling me close to pin my hands between us.

"We did frantic this morning," he reminded me, his voice a caress against my ear as he slid his hands to the hem of my sweater and pulled. It came over my head, and I reached up to release my hair from the elastic I'd caged it in. Alec looked down, his big hands cupping my breasts over the lacy red bra. "Tonight, I want to savor you."

He leaned down, pressing a kiss to the top of one breast, then the other, as his thumbs swept over the delicate lace. I cursed myself that I hadn't worn the matching panties as he made shivers pebble the skin across my stomach, but he hadn't seemed to mind much this morning.

"You're beautiful, Sage," he murmured, his eyes drinking in my still mostly clothed body as his fingers went to the button of my slacks. He flicked it open, tugging them down and helping me step out of them as he sucked in a breath. "Pure magic."

"I don't match," I said, feeling suddenly shy under his scrutiny. "The panties—"

"Are fucking perfect," he growled, his hands searing a heated path over my waist to my backside. He squeezed, a teasing touch that had me gripping his arms tightly. "I like the little reindeer on them," he added, flicking the waistband of my Christmassy underwear. "I'll be keeping them as a trophy."

"You will not," I said, laughing as I reached for the buttons on his shirt and tugged the first few open. "Your turn, now."

"Not yet." He stilled my hands, stepping into me and pressing a kiss to the place my neck met my shoulder as he unhooked my bra. "I told you, I'm savoring."

He pulled me down to the bed with him, his body atop mine as he peppered a trail of kisses from my shoulder to my now bare breasts to my navel. He slid down, ending up on his knees before my open thighs.

"You don't have to—"

"Sage," he said, using his Dr. Ashcroft voice as he slid the panties down, baring me to him completely. I bit my lower lip as he looked his fill, his gaze hungry and heated as he took in all of me. He met my eyes again, and they blazed with a fire I hadn't seen before. "No more talking now."

With a quick yank, he pulled me to the end of the bed and pressed his mouth to me.

I gasped, the feel of his tongue hot against me as he parted me with soft, teasing strokes. Gods above, I was going to combust.

How did this man so utterly undo me? How had I spent so long loathing him when now I liked him very, very much?

"Stop thinking, Sage," he chastised, using a hand to press my pelvis firmly against the bed as he returned to his place between my thighs, licking tiny circles as he explored me.

"I will when you do," I breathed, feeling a heady combination of magic and desire flood my veins as I inadvertently drew power from the leyline.

I cursed. It had been years since I'd lost control like that during sex, a sign of just how thoroughly Alec undid me.

I channeled the power into something harmless as I released the magic in a gentle flurry of snow that melted as it hit the ground and my overheated skin.

Alec laughed, and the sound vibrated through me as he brushed the snow from my abdomen and legs, continuing to lick and suck and explore parts of me that few men had taken time to investigate.

I moaned, unable to resist moving my hips as release grew closer, and Alec skimmed one hand up my body to tease my nipples. He made a noise of satisfaction against me as he slid two fingers in, finding me soaked. I clamped down on him in release, crying out as I fisted the blankets beneath me.

He continued his attention on me, building a second climax so soon after the first, it left me boneless and shaking on the bed.

"I will never get tired of how you taste," he declared, pressing gentle kisses to my inner thigh and knee as he rose, lips slightly glossy, and drew his fingers into his mouth.

"Get down here," I commanded, reaching up to pull him to me.

He crawled over me, still fully clothed, and kissed me as I pulled at his shirt. It came over his head, and I attacked his buckle next. He laughed, rising onto his knees to help me as my fingers still shook with the aftermath of the orgasms he had given me.

"Move faster," I begged, lying propped up on my elbows behind me as I watched him undress, my eyes shooting to the bulge that betrayed his own arousal.

"Impatient," Alec chastised, earning a frustrated growl from me and smirking like he knew exactly what the waiting was doing to me. "I still have to decide how I want you. Beneath me?" He knelt on the bed, fully naked and erect, pumping himself once. "Above me?" He crawled over me, his length sliding up my body as he leaned down to kiss me again. "Sitting on my face?"

I whimpered a little as he nuzzled my breasts, flicking a tongue over each pert nipple.

He laughed, bringing his eyes back to my face. "There are so very many options."

"Hurry up and pick one," I urged, trying to pull him atop me and make the decision for him.

He gripped me tightly, flipping us suddenly so he was under me, and I sat up to straddle him.

"I think I want to watch you ride me first," he said, smirking in a very male way as he braced my hips and aligned us. "Last chance to back out, Sage."

In answer, I leaned down, kissing him soundly as I lowered myself onto him. He speared inside me, groaning as I took him to the hilt.

"You were saying?" I murmured, biting his lower lip and tugging gently as he rocked his hips beneath me.

"Fuck, Sage," he groaned, threading his fingers through my hair with one hand and grasping my hip with the other. "You feel..."

"Like magic?" I suggested, kissing his nose and tapping into the leyline on purpose this time to sprinkle him with snow.

He yelped at the sudden cold, then growled and began to drive into me. His hips thrust up to meet mine, and he took my breast in his mouth, sucking mercilessly until I felt the other one ache with need. He switched sides as if sensing my desire, pulling my hips to meet his every thrust as he brought us both closer to the edge.

"Just like magic," he breathed, flipping us again so I was on my back and he could get the leverage he needed to find his release. He buried his face in my neck, holding me tightly as he drove into me. Pleasure shot up my spine as the friction and tension coiled and grew.

He shouted his release, sending me over the edge with him as he shuddered into me.

After several long moments breathing each other in, Alec lifted his head. His eyes met mine, shining with warmth and disbelief. "That was..."

"Magical?" I teased, earning a nip on the nose as Alec rolled to the side and pulled me with him, settling me into the crook of his arm. My head fit perfectly into the hollow between his neck and shoulder, and I melted into him as he settled a blanket over us and kissed the top of my head.

"Definitely magical," he agreed, running his fingers in soothing strokes down my arm. "I'm securely under your spell."

"I didn't pin you as one for cheesy romantic lines," I teased, kissing his chest and smiling against him.

"Oh, I'm the worst," he joked, squeezing me against him. "Literally, every cliché in the book is about to come out of my mouth."

"Hmm." I lifted my chin to rest on his chest and meet his gaze. His eyes were fixed on me with a mix of adoration and wonder and need. No man had ever looked at me like Alec Ashcroft did, and it hit me that I'd actually seen him look at me the same way before. "When did you know you wanted me?"

"Who says I want you?" he teased, earning a poke in the ribs. "Ow, mercy," he laughed, nipping my nose to stop my assault. "I think if I had to date it, it would be Halloween, your first year in the lab."

"Halloween?" I asked, surprised by this answer. "Why Halloween?"

"You were wearing a ridiculous Hocus Pocus sweater that read 'I smell children,' and I thought it was the most adorable thing in the world," he replied, raising a brow at me as he smiled.

"*That* did it for you?" I asked skeptically. I remembered that sweater, and it definitely *was not* sexy. How could that possibly be when he knew?

"It's when you first brought Binx to the lab," he continued, stroking my back idly. "And I remember thinking that this girl was so perfect, she must be a gift of fate."

"You *really* like Hocus Pocus, huh?" I asked, earning a poke in my own ribs.

"I really like *you*," Alec corrected, pressing his nose to mine. "That just convinced me that you had good taste. The rest of my infatuation with you came on slowly over the three years we worked together."

My stomach rumbled so loudly at that moment that we both burst out laughing. Alec retrieved reheated stew, and we ate in bed while discussing movies and books we liked. I described my family and how I got into portomancy, and an hour later I was yawning as Alec tucked me into his side to sleep.

"Merry Christmas, Sage," he murmured, pressing his lips to my temple and squeezing me tighter.

"Merry Christmas, Alec," I whispered.

Something in me flooded with affection, and I made myself a silent promise as we drifted off to sleep that Alec would never be alone for Christmas again.

Chapter 10

CHRISTMAS DAY

I WOKE IN ALEC'S arms, Binx meowing loudly at the foot of the bed as morning light streamed in through the window.

"Five more minutes," I groaned, pulling a pillow over my head to block out Binx's whining.

"Tell your wretched cat that it's Christmas," Alec grumbled, stealing my pillow from me to place over his own head. "We get to sleep in."

I gasped, sitting up and throwing the pillow off Alec. "It's Christmas!"

"Sage," Alec groaned, pulling me back down so my face was close to his, our noses nearly touching. He pulled the pillow over us. "Sleep now, Christmas later."

His lips brushed mine. His face was slightly spiky from three days of stubble in a way I didn't hate. His hands moved over my waist, and I was certain that sleep was out of the question as he pulled me against him and deepened the kiss.

"I can't breathe under here," I laughed, pushing the pillow away and making him hiss like a vampire exposed to sunlight. I laughed again, wrapping a blanket around my still-naked body. "And Binx and Max are mewling outside."

"Cursed familiars," he groaned, heaving himself out of bed, half hard and looking at me like he might be wholly hard in a moment.

"None of that," I said, pointing to his groin. "Christmas first. I know there won't be any presents, but I have traditions."

"Fine," Alec sighed, tying a blanket around his waist like an oversized kilt and putting his arms around me. He kissed my cheek. "What traditions?"

"Well, we always have cocoa and open presents in pajamas," I said, looking down and blushing faintly.

"The pajamas are a lost cause," he laughed, kissing my other cheek. It was like he couldn't stop now that he had started, and I felt the same way. It had been two days of fooling around and only three of not actively hating him, but somehow, this thing between us felt right. Natural. We'd probably have to have a conversation about what we were now exactly, but it could wait. "But we can manage the cocoa. What else?"

"Mom usually makes Christmas waffles," I hedged, trying to remember if I had seen waffle mix in the enchanted kitchen. I had no idea how to make waffles from scratch. "With whipped cream and peppermint sprinkles."

"That will be harder to manage," Alec said thoughtfully, weaving his fingers into my hair and massaging my scalp gently. Binx let out a piteous whine behind the door, and he rolled his eyes. "Anything else?"

"Yes, but it's silly," I said, giving him a wry smile. "Dr. Alec Ashcroft may not be up for Christmas silliness."

"With you?" Alec asked, grinning down at me so that both dimples made an appearance. "Try me."

"Well, Mom and Dad always share a Christmas kiss after opening presents and before making breakfast," I explained, thinking of how happy this silly little tradition made both of my parents. "My dad picks my mom up and spins her while kissing under the mistletoe."

Alec leaned down, brushing his lips over mine while smiling. It made heat pool low in my core, and little bolts of anticipatory pleasure flashed through my sensitive places. "I think that can be arranged," he murmured.

"Good," I said a little breathlessly. "Then I'll find something to feed Binx."

"I thought presents were first?" Alec said, scooping me up in his arms. I yelped, surprised but delighted at being held so tightly by him.

"I can walk now," I protested, contradicting myself by winding my arms tightly around his neck. "You fixed me, remember?"

"But I like holding you," Alec teased, kicking open the bedroom door and carrying me bridal-style through the cold kitchen. I shivered, and he chuckled. "I like keeping you warm."

"I can think of other ways for you to keep me warm," I suggested, feeling suddenly ridiculous for insisting on tradition when I had a sexy wizard eager to engage in other activities. "Plus, there aren't any presents."

"I think I heard Santa last night," Alec said cryptically, settling me on the couch as he moved to light a fire in the big stone fireplace. "You'd better check your stocking."

He lifted one of the knitted stockings off a hook and tossed it to me. I caught it as Binx and Max scrambled onto the couch to complain at me.

"We've been trapped here for three days," I said, squeezing the bottom of the stocking. There was something malleable inside, and I frowned at Alec.

"It's a placeholder gift," he said, shrugging as he turned from the now blazing fire to join me on the couch. He had a second stocking with him, and a mischievous look on his face. "Seems like Santa left something for me, too."

"You don't have to—"

He interrupted me with a kiss, only pulling away when I melted into him enough to not argue. "Open your present, Sage."

I stuck my hand in the stocking, closing it around something soft. I pulled out a pair of hand-knitted socks with a pattern of red snowflakes around the ankle.

"They were my mom's," Alec said when I looked up at him in question. He pulled a second pair from his own stocking, green with little pine trees around them. His smile was a little sad as he added, "And my dad's. But it's cold, and I figured she would want us to have them."

He pulled on the socks, dropping the blanket, and turning in a circle for my inspection, completely naked aside from the knitted masterpieces.

I laughed, pulling his mom's pair over my own cold toes and holding them out for his approval.

"Perfect," he said, pulling me to my feet and throwing a blanket around both of us. "Now we're cozy."

"Are you sure?" I asked, looking up at him with concern thumping in my heart. It felt important and a little scary, accepting a piece of his mother from him like this.

"She would have loved you," he said, taking my hands in his between us. "As much as I love you."

I looked up in surprise, but he kissed me fiercely before I could respond.

"You don't have to say it back," he murmured, one hand splaying possessively over my back as the other cupped the back of my head, the blanket slipping down around us. "I know it's too soon to say it, but it's the truth. It's been the truth for the last three years."

"It has?" I asked, meeting his big, anxious eyes as I tried to think over our interactions and assess how I had missed his feelings for me. Nothing stood out at first in my mind, but I remembered a few lingering looks I had written off as critical, shift changes I was sure were arranged to irritate me, peer review meetings that lasted far longer than any of the other grad students. "Why did you wait so long to say anything?"

He sighed, dropping his forehead to mine. "Because I've lost everyone I've ever loved, Sage," he said finally. "And I didn't want to risk losing you, too. Better to have you close, even if it meant you hating me, than risk letting you go."

"Gods, Alec," I murmured, kissing his bare chest. "For such a smart man, you certainly are an idiot sometimes."

"What?" He laughed, looking at me with a raised brow.

"If you had said something, we might have had years of this!" I exclaimed, gesturing to the cabin and our nakedness as the blanket fell completely away. I shivered at the heated look he gave me.

"Would you have gone out with me?" he asked incredulously, his expression a mix of exasperation and amusement. "Really? It took being accidentally transported to an isolated cabin in a blizzard via an unstable portal for you and I to even be civil to each other."

"I mean, maybe," I hedged. "If you'd been a bit less cold and a bit more like *this* Alec."

"*This* Alec was always there," he said, cupping my face with his hands and running his thumbs gently over my cheeks. "But, perhaps he wasn't ready for you yet."

"Perhaps," I agreed, closing my eyes as the tension melted from me with his gentle touch. "Perhaps it was this *Sage* who wasn't ready for *him*."

He responded to me fiercely, pulling me flush against him and kissing me senseless, his tongue sweeping over mine as he poured three years of longing into me.

It didn't matter that it was far too soon or that rogue magic had made it happen. What I felt for Alec was real, and terrifying, and exciting, and I wanted to explore it. I wanted to watch Hocus Pocus with him on Halloween, and introduce him to my sisters, and share our research, and a thousand other little moments I had never wanted with anyone else.

When we broke apart, I was gasping for breath, and he was grinning like an idiot. "I knew I'd win you over."

"Gods, you did not," I argued, laughing as he lifted me and spun me around, kissing me once more.

"Presents," he said, finally putting me down, "and Christmas kiss complete. What's next?"

Binx meowed, adamant that next should be his breakfast, but a roaring outside made both of us start. I grabbed the blanket, throwing it around myself as Alec did the same.

"What in the—"

"Sage!" came a chorus of voices, all shouting my name in different tones above the roaring noise outside.

Alec raised a brow at me, going to investigate. I followed, curiously looking over his shoulder as he opened the door to the frozen winter outside.

A female voice shrieked, and he shut the door quickly, turning his back against it as he faced me with a scowl.

"I think your family is here."

Epilogue

Two Weeks After Christmas

"It's very impressive work, Miss Bishop," Dr. Dvaran said across his oak desk, flipping through the pages of my translations as his bushy white mustache twitched.

Alec was likely waiting outside the door like he'd threatened. I smiled thinking about his messy hair that he was probably making messier with his anxiety.

He had been a good sport about my family showing up in a rented snow plow, presents and waffle mix in tow, and insistent on having our usual family Christmas. My note had arrived, and they had taken it upon themselves to rescue us.

Dad and Mom had taken our nakedness in stride, Mom suggesting gently that we both get dressed for breakfast while Willow and Paisley made lewd gestures behind her back.

Dad had joined in, to my mortification.

Once we were decent for company, the smell of waffles and hot cocoa filled the little cabin. Mom had even brought presents for Alec, knowing he was trapped with me, and he made a good show of thanking her for the fancy pens and other stationery my mom seemed to think postdocs might need.

He barely took his eyes off me the whole morning, and when we packed up the cabin to leave with my family, he held my hand tightly as if afraid I would evaporate like a dream.

"I'm not going anywhere," I told him from the privacy of my childhood bedroom once we arrived at my parents' house. I had insisted Alec stay for at least the night rather than heading back to his lonely apartment at the Academy. My mom had fussed a bit at him sharing my room until my dad reminded her that they'd found us extremely naked, and it likely wouldn't be the first time.

My flaming embarrassment could have melted the entire mountainside on which the cabin stood.

"I know," Alec replied, speaking low despite the sound shield he'd cast on the door when locking it behind him. "I know, it's just..."

"You thought we had more time before reality crept back in?" I asked, smiling and rising on my toes to kiss him. I was still wearing the knitted socks, and there really was something magically warm about them.

"I did," Alec confessed, dropping his forehead to mine. "I'm not sure I'm ready to share you just yet."

"I'm afraid you don't have much of a choice," I sighed, working the buttons on his flannel shirt open. "Now, help me defile my old bedroom."

"Miss Bishop?" Dr. Dvaran said, pulling me from the memory of Alec's bare chest surrounded by my pink bedspread that made my thighs clench.

"Sorry," I said, smiling at my advisor. "So, will I get to defend it early?"

"I think so," Dr. Dvaran said, flicking the file closed on a puff of air pulled from one of the hundreds of leylines that converged beneath us. "Once you do, I'd like to talk to you about your future prospects here. There's a faculty position that I think might help you further your research."

"Oh," I said, feigning surprise and beaming. "I thought Casimir—"

"Dr. Flint has been suspended pending a thorough ethics review," Dr. Dvaran said, his voice heavy with disdain. "I doubt he will be returning to the department." He stood, his sign that I was dismissed, as he held out a hand to me. I shook it, and he offered me a rare smile. "Normally I wouldn't say this until after a successful defense, but I'm looking forward to having you on board, *Dr.* Bishop."

"Thank you, sir," I said, trying not to squeal with excitement as I left his office, opening the door with magic as if it were nothing. While the cabin had been an exceptional sort of accident, it was glorious to have access to proper magic again.

"Oh, and Dr. Bishop?" Dr. Dvaran said, stopping me as I was halfway out the door. He gave me an exasperated look, his bushy white eyebrows rising. "Please tell Dr. Ashcroft to stop hovering outside my door. Take your boyfriend with you when you go."

"Yes, sir," I said, smiling as I shut the door and found Alec leaning guiltily against the wall.

"Well?" he asked, pushing off from the wall and falling into step next to me. We had been cautious about seeming overly familiar at work, but clearly, we hadn't been wholly successful if Dr. Dvaran had figured it out.

"He wants to talk to me about the job after my dissertation defense," I said, biting my lip to stop my face from splitting apart with the grin I felt rising in me. "He called me Dr. Bishop."

Alec whooped—a real, actual, joyful whoop—and lifted me, spinning me in a very un-Dr. Ashcroft sort of way. Heedless of watching eyes or the undergrads in the lower lab or the postdocs grabbing their eighteenth cup of coffee, he kissed me right there in the middle of the hallway for everyone to see.

"Stuck with me for a while then," he teased, finally putting me down as I tried to rearrange my ponytail into something resembling professionalism. "How ever will you cope?"

"I'll find a way," I quipped, bumping his hip with mine as we continued back to the portomancy lab. "The real question is how will *you* cope? You're going to be seeing me morning, afternoon, and night."

"I will?" he asked, frowning down at me, the collar of his flannel shirt sticking up over the collar of his robes. I paused, smiling as I smoothed it down and kissed him gently.

"When I move in, of course," I said, answering the question he had asked me this morning when I was half asleep and barely able to function. He widened his eyes, then beamed down at me, Max poking out of his pocket in excitement.

"You'll have to put up a Christmas tree next year, though," I warned, taking his arm and guiding him back to the lab, where I fully intended we explore the universes together. "And just wait until you see me at Halloween."

"I'll find a way to manage," he said. He took my face in his hands and kissed me again as the rest of the lab gaped at us. "As long as I get to be with you, we can hex the blasted halls as much as you like."

About the Author

MADELEINE ELIOT

Madeleine Eliot loves to read and write spicy romantasy with all of the best tropes. Dubbed the "Queen of Cozy" by her readers, Madeleine enjoys writing romantasy that is all vibes and spice, with a dash of adventure and world-building. She is always working on her next book, which is probably another spicy romantasy. Follow her adventures and latest works at instagram.com/made leineeliotwrites

Also By Madeleine Eliot

Queen of All Fae Series

A Dream of Stars and Darkness

A Dream of Earth and Ash

A Dream of Frost and Fury

A Dream of Sun and Solstice (Novella)

King and Coven Series

To Hunt a Demon King

To Break a Demon Curse

To Claim a Daemon Lord (Novella)

To Wear a Demon Crown

To Sway a Demon Heart (Novella)

It's Beginning to Look a Lot Like Witches

Hex the Halls

The Whispering Sea Duet

Ballad of Sea and Sky
Hymn of Breath and Bone

Enchanted Hearts Series

Gold & Shadow
Blood & Roses
Glass & Charms (Releasing 2025)
Vine & Violence (Release Date TBA)
Hush & Whispers (Release Date TBA)
Frost & Crystal (Release Date TBA)
Dreams & Briars (Release Date TBA)

Printed in Great Britain
by Amazon

59014400R00061